LITTLE BLUE
ALIEN

Written by
KATE RUTTLE

Illustrated by
ELEFTHERIA-GARYFALLIA
LEFTHERI

WAYLAND

First published in 2011
by Wayland

Text copyright © Kate Ruttle 2011

Illustration copyright © Wayland 2011

Wayland
338 Euston Road
London NW1 3BH

Wayland Australia
Level 17/207 Kent Street
Sydney, NSW 2000

Series editor: Louise John
Editor: Katie Woolley
Designer: Paul Cherrill
Consultant: Kate Ruttle

A CIP catalogue record for this book is available
from the British Library.

ISBN 9780750263917

Printed in China

Wayland is a division of Hachette Children's Books,
an Hachette UK company. www.hachette.co.uk

All photos © Shutterstock, with the exception of the
swing and slide on page 16 and the net on page 18.

FIZZ WIZZ PHONICS is a series of fun and exciting books, especially designed to be used by children who have not yet started to read.

The books support the development of language, exploring key speaking and listening skills, as well as encouraging confidence in pre-reading skills.

LITTLE BLUE ALIEN is all about oral blending. Blending is an important skill that children need in order to begin to start reading. Blending happens when you see or hear a string of individual sounds and you **blend** (combine) them together to make a word. When doing blending activities with children, it is important to recognise the number of sounds and not the number of letters in the word, for example sh~ee~p has three sounds and not six.

This book encourages children to begin to hear the individual sounds in words. Throughout the book, Zog the alien speaks in sounds. When you read Zog's speech aloud with your child, say the sounds you can hear in the words, for example the sounds in 'spoon' are s~p~oo~n.

Try to read Zog's speech in an alien voice, and encourage your child to do the same. Children will enjoy learning that words are made up of sounds, and blending the sounds together.

For suggestions on how to use **LITTLE BLUE ALIEN** and for further activities, look at page 24 of this book.

Bump! A loud noise woke Yan up.
She crept downstairs and opened
the back door.

"H~e~ll~o," said a little blue alien.
"I am Z~o~g."

Blend:
b~ir~d is **bird**
c~a~t is **cat**
d~o~g is **dog**

Zog was visiting Earth to look
at lots of different things.
"What do you want to see?" asked Yan.

Zog showed Yan some photographs.
"B~ir~d, c~a~t, d~o~g!" he cried.

Blend:
c~u~p is **cup**
s~p~oo~n is **spoon**
b~ow~l is **bowl**

At breakfast time, Zog showed Yan
and Dad some more photographs.
"That's a cup, a spoon and a bowl!" said Yan.

8

Zog pointed to Dad's breakfast.
"C~u~p, s~p~oo~n, b~ow~l!" said Zog.

After breakfast, Dad and Yan got ready to go out. It was a windy day so Yan put on her scarf, coat and hat.

Zog was excited and pointed to Yan.
"S~c~ar~f, c~oa~t, h~a~t!" he cried.

Blend:
c~ar is **car**
b~i~ke is **bike**
t~r~u~ck is **truck**

Then Zog, Yan and Dad went outside.
Zog wanted to see even more things.
"This is Dad's car," said Yan.

Zog, Yan and Dad drove down the street.
"C~ar, b~i~ke, t~r~u~ck!" shouted Zog.

Blend:
m~ea~t is **meat**
b~r~ea~d is **bread**
e~gg~s is **eggs**

At the supermarket, Zog was surprised to see all the food. The people were even more surprised to see an alien out shopping!

"What shall we look at first?" asked Dad.
"M~ea~t, b~r~ea~d, e~gg~s!" said Zog.

After all the shopping, Dad took Yan and Zog to the park.
"Shall we feed the ducks?" asked Yan.

But Zog thought the slide was more fun!
"D~u~ck~s, s~w~i~ng, s~l~i~de!"
he yelled.

Later on, Ben came round to play.
Zog showed him some photographs, too.
"That's called a ball," said Ben.

Yan, Zog and Ben went outside to play football.
"B~a~ll, n~e~t, g~oa~l!" cried Zog.

When Ben went home, it was time for tea.
Zog showed Mum what he wanted to eat.
"Ok, let's have fish and chips!" said Mum.

For pudding, there was a chocolate cake.
"F~i~sh, ch~i~p~s, c~a~ke,"
laughed Zog.

Blend:
m~oo~n is **moon**
s~t~ar~s is **stars**
h~o~me is **home**

After tea, Zog was tired. He had
some last photographs to show.
"Is it time to go home, Zog?" asked Dad.